"I want to hear about your life since we last saw each other,"

Tony said. He seemed to hesitate for a moment.

Natalie's pulse began to race. Was this actually happening? Did Tony want to see her again, to spend time with her, after all that had happened between them?

Was there such a thing as a second chance?

"That would be fine," she heard herself saying, then considered what she was doing to herself. This was going to be some kind of refined torture.

Torture or not, she couldn't resist. How could anyone resist magic?

ANNETTE BROADRICK

Christmas Magic

SILHOUETTE BOOKS
300 E. 42nd St., New York, N.Y. 10017

ISBN: 0-373-48217-5

CHRISTMAS MAGIC
Copyright © 1988 by Annette Broadrick
Originally published in
Silhouette Christmas Stories 1988
Copyright © 1988 by Silhouette Books

Printed in the U.S.A.

Christmas Magic

Dear Reader:

We asked our editors to find us something really special as a holiday gift for our Reader Service members, and they've created this volume just for you.

It's our Christmas present to you, a small token of appreciation for being a loyal reader and for allowing us into your life...and into your heart.

Annette Broadrick, a favorite author of ours, has written a Christmas romance, the story of two people who renew their love during the holiday season.

We hope you'll enjoy it and accept our sincere wishes for a Merry Christmas and a Happy New Year.

Candy Lee
Reader Service

Chapter One

Natalie Phillips patiently made her way through the crush of Christmas shoppers in the large department store. The store and the mall surrounding it had been built during the six years since Natalie had left Portland, Oregon. This was the first time she had returned to the city where she'd grown up, and thus far she had found the visit to be as painful as she had feared it would be. Poignant memories kept intruding on the present.

In quiet desperation, Natalie had borrowed her brother's car that afternoon and had gone shopping at the Clackamas Town Center, a large mall near I-205. Surely she would find nothing there to remind her of other times—of happier and more innocent times.

Natalie had learned a great deal about people in the six years she had been gone. Never would she be so gullible again, so willing to believe in fantasies—in happy-ever-after.

She could sense the anticipation and excitement in the very air she breathed. Christmastime—a time to spend with loved ones; a time of suppressed excitement and secrets; a time of smiles and laughter, of family warmth and giving; a time of peace.

Unfortunately Natalie hadn't been able to find much peace. Not in Portland. She had another life now and no longer wanted any reminders of the past. She had left the unhappiness of six years ago behind her and was determined not to allow it to influence her future.

Natalie watched as a young child paused to exclaim over a Christmas display at the store's wide entrance to the rest of the mall. The excited child pointed, calling his mother's attention to the glitter and animated figures.

Natalie glanced around, unconsciously searching for someone with whom she could share the small scene. Her gaze caught and held for a moment, and she stared at the broad back of a man standing in front of a jewelry display counter.

There was something about the wide shoulders, the confident stance and the way he held his head that reminded her of the one man she had worked hard to forget.

Tony D'Angelo.

Surely not. She must be imagining a likeness that wasn't there. After all, she hadn't seen him in six years. No doubt the Tony she remembered no longer existed. He had probably never been as attractive as her memory had recalled during the many nights she'd lain awake thinking about him.

Natalie moved closer, drawn to the man who seemed to be intently studying the jewelry beneath the glass display counter. He turned his head so that she saw his profile, and Natalie froze, no longer able to deny what her senses were telling her.

There was no mistaking that beautiful profile that looked as though it belonged on an ancient Roman coin. Black curly hair fell across his forehead, and he impatiently shoved it back, a familiar gesture that almost brought tears to her eyes.

Hesitantly, Natalie cut through the crowd toward him. Should she speak to him? Would he even remember her? Wouldn't it be better to leave all of her fantasies and memories intact? Surely speaking to him would only destroy any of her remaining illusions.

But could she walk away and not at least give herself the opportunity to speak to him once more? While part of her seemed to be in a perpetual debate, her feet continued to move toward him until she stood an arm's length away.

"Tony?"

She watched as he seemed to tense, then slowly turned to face her.

"I wasn't sure it was you," she said, trying to smile. "Hello, Tony."

The six years had been more than kind to him. His body had matured and filled out. At twenty-two he had been tall and slender with a wiry strength that she'd found impressive. Now his arms and chest were wide, tapering down to a narrow waist and hips.

His face looked more chiseled. There were lines around his mouth and eyes that hadn't been there before. And his eyes—those beautifully expressive black eyes—no longer told Natalie what he was thinking. He stared at her with no discernible expression.

"Don't you remember me? I'm Natalie—"

"I remember you," he broke in. "I was just surprised to see you."

"Yes. It's been a long time, hasn't it?"

"Has it?"

His gaze flickered over her as though automatically registering any changes in her. She wondered what he would see. She had just turned eighteen the last time she had seen him. She'd been so young then—too young to have known how to handle the situation she'd found herself in. Would she ever be able to forget the last time she'd seen him? He'd been angry then, watching her with snapping eyes as she'd walked away—out of his life and away from the future that they had naively planned together.

It was obvious he'd never forgiven her for her behavior. Those expressive black eyes were now shuttered, reflecting nothing of his thoughts or feelings.

"Do you live around—" Natalie started to say when someone brushed heavily against her and knocked her off balance and against Tony. She stumbled, and he automatically put his arms around her to keep her from falling.

Being suddenly jarred was not responsible for the way her body reacted to his touch. How many nights had she dreamed of being in Tony's arms once more, of having him hold her close, murmuring soft love words in her ear? How could she ever forget the hard-muscled length of him, the familiar scent of his after-shave lotion that continued to haunt her whenever she caught a whiff of it being worn by someone else—and the way she fit so well against him, her head nestling into his shoulder?

Natalie placed her hands on his chest and tried to collect herself. "I'm sorry," she muttered breathlessly. "I'm afraid—"

He cut her off by growling, "Let's get out of here." Taking her arm he guided her out of the store and across the mall to the ice-skating area. Food franchises circled the upper level, and he moved with her toward the small tables and chairs that overlooked the rink. Motioning for her to sit down, he asked, "What would you like to drink?"

In some respects Tony hadn't changed. He was still in charge, not even asking if she wanted something— just giving her a choice. Six years ago he probably wouldn't have bothered asking that—he would have known her so well he would have automatically ordered for her.

"A hot chocolate, please," she said, and met his gaze.

She saw his eyes flicker briefly at her familiar selection, then whatever emotion had washed over him was gone. "I'll be right back."

Natalie watched as Tony weaved his way through the crowd to the nearest window and ordered.

Now that she could catch her breath, Natalie observed other changes in him, changes that surprised her.

His clothes, for one thing. Tony had always worn jeans, motorcycle boots and a black leather jacket, only one of the many reasons her father had disapproved of him. She smiled at the memory. She remembered how her heart would race whenever she heard the sound of his motorcycle pulling into the driveway.

Even then Tony hadn't cared what anyone thought of him, not even her father. He had dressed the way he wanted.

He'd worked in construction back then, and his wardrobe hadn't lent itself to formal attire. Tony had worked hard—doing heavy physical labor, taking on tasks that others shirked.

Whatever he was doing now for a living was certainly not hard on his clothes. He wore well-fitting slacks that accented his hips and thighs and a pull-over sweater that made a pleasing contrast to the long-sleeved shirt he wore.

But no tie.

That was in keeping with the Tony she remembered. She continued to watch him through the crowd as he patiently waited in line. Patience had never been one of Tony's biggest virtues, either.

But then she'd never considered patience particularly appealing herself. Yet now she was content to sit and watch him, speculating on his life in the past few years.

Was he married? He didn't wear any rings, but then he'd once explained to her that rings were dangerous in his business. Maybe he'd never gotten into the habit of wearing one.

Natalie had long ago convinced herself that she would not get upset when the time came that she heard Tony D'Angelo had married someone else. How could she possibly blame him? If she hadn't been so frightened and so unsure of herself, perhaps she could have better withstood her father's terrible anger.

She shook her head. Dwelling on the past was such a waste of time. There was no way to go back to undo the damage that had been done. Instead she forced herself to bring her mind back to the present and to the fact that, despite everything that had happened between them, she could think of no one she'd rather be with. For a short space out of time, Natalie was reminded of the magic of Christmas, the magic that Tony D'Angelo had brought into her life so many years before.

To most people, Natalie Phillips's childhood would have seemed to be blessed with a plentiful supply of wealth and advantages. Her brother, ten years older, had never had much time for her, and her mother had been very cautious about her playmates.

Consequently she had been a rather lonely child. She'd learned early in life to amuse herself by reading or playing with her dolls. Later she had enjoyed swimming and tennis, whenever she could find someone who was willing to play.

Natalie could remember exactly when she first laid eyes on Tony. She'd been ten years old.

It was summertime, and she had spent the morning in the house. She'd been upset that day, she remembered, because her parents had refused to allow her to go to summer camp. Or more precisely, her father had refused. Her mother had acquiesced to his decision as she always had, even though she had better understood Natalie's desire to go.

Henry Phillips had learned early in life that his only vulnerability was through his family, and he guarded them jealously. He knew that he'd stepped on many people getting to the top. He'd made enemies. He didn't care, but he wasn't going to take any chances that his family would suffer for any of his decisions. Consequently, Natalie was given very little freedom.

That day she had felt rebellious at her father's restrictions and had stomped outside, looking for a way to vent her anger and frustration.

Instead, she had fallen in love.

Fourteen-year-old Tony was riding a large lawn mower in the area behind her home. Two men were trimming the hedge that surrounded the swimming pool, but she never even noticed them.

He wore a pair of cutoffs that left his bronzed body bare. A red bandanna tied around his head kept his hair and the perspiration out of his face. He was so intent on what he was doing that he was oblivious to the people around him.

He looked like Adonis to the impressionable Natalie. She lost track of time as she watched him. Eventually the heat of the day penetrated her preoccupation. That's when she came up with the idea of bringing the gardeners something to drink.

Natalie rushed into the house, made a pitcher of ice water, found some freshly baked cookies and hastily returned to the back lawn.

Tony had stopped the mower and was checking the grass catcher when she came out.

"Hi! I bet you're thirsty, aren't you? I brought you some water and some cookies," she said.

She would never forget the way he had turned around, looked at her standing there so eagerly holding the tray and smiled.

"That sounds great. Thanks." She watched him untie the bandanna and rub it over his face before re-tying it around his forehead. Then he walked over to where she had set the tray on one of the tables by the pool. "What's your name?" he asked with a grin, af-ter promptly emptying one of the glasses.

"Natalie."

"Thanks for the water, Natalie. That was very thoughtful of you." He glanced over at the house. "You live there?"

She nodded.

"Nice place," he said, studying the lines of the house as though they meant something to him.

"Would those men like something to drink?" she asked, nodding to the men who were at the far end of the pool.

"I'm sure they would." He raised his voice. "Say, Uncle Pietro, do you and Grandpapa want some wa-ter?"

The younger man glanced up. "We have a jug of water, Tony, and you know it. Don't bother the little girl."

Natalie flushed.

Tony glanced around and grinned. "He's right, but the ice has long since melted. And we certainly didn't bring any cookies!"

His black eyes danced mischievously as though she would understand and share the joke.

"How old are you, Natalie?" he asked, after he'd finished off two of the cookies.

"Ten."

"Ah, that's a good age."

"How old are you?"

"Fourteen."

"I'll be glad when I'm fourteen!"

"Why?"

"Because then maybe my father will let me do more things. He never lets me go anywhere!"

Tony smiled. "Maybe he just wants to protect you."

"From what?"

"From the world. From life. You're a very pretty girl, Natalie. If you were mine, I'd want to protect you, too."

His flashing smile in his dark face caused her breath to catch in her throat. He thought she was pretty? He would want to protect her, too?

She smiled, unable to think of anything to say.

"Get back to work, Tony. We don't have all day," one of the men hollered.

Tony shrugged and grinned. "I gotta run. Thanks again, Natalie."

She had watched him as he'd walked away with a spring to his step. She remembered thinking that day that she had never met anyone like him. She found him fascinating.

Nothing had ever caused her to change her mind.

"Here you are."

Startled, Natalie glanced up to see Tony sitting down across from her at the table. He carried two steaming insulated paper cups.

"It's good to see you again, Tony," she managed to say, her voice sounding husky to her ears.

He sat there for a few moments in silence, studying her. Finally he spoke. "Six years is a long time, isn't it?"

"Yes."

"You look very different from the young girl I watched grow up. I didn't think you could ever be more beautiful than you were at eighteen. I was wrong."

He spoke in a quiet, matter-of-fact tone, as though he were discussing the weather or skiing conditions on Mount Hood. He was making it clear that no matter how he'd reacted to her in the past, she had no effect on him now.

"How have you been, Tony?"

He took a sip of his drink. "You're a little late in asking, aren't you?"

"Yes, I suppose I am. I have no excuses to make for my behavior back then. I behaved very badly."

"Not really. You were young. You'd been sheltered all your life. Your actions were predictable."

"Perhaps. But I can see that you never forgave me for leaving."

"It wasn't a matter of forgiveness. You made your choice, that's all."

They sat there for a few moments in silence, sipping their hot drinks. Natalie discovered that she couldn't meet his gaze. She recalled that he had always had a direct gaze. He'd stood up to her father and brother, never showing any sign of being intimidated by them. Natalie had always felt as though Tony had the ability to look deep inside her, to see her innermost thoughts and feelings.

If only she had the knack of doing the same thing with him.

"How's your family?" she finally asked.

"Fine. Mama is busy cooking and baking for the holidays." He shook his head. "Now Angela is working right along with her. They could feed everyone around us for blocks."

"Is Angela married?"

He tilted his head slightly. "As a matter of fact, she is. Why?"

"I just wondered. I wrote to her a couple of times after I went back East to school. But she never answered." Natalie shrugged. "I've wondered if she decided to go on to school."

"Yes, she did. She met Paul in one of her classes. They were married two years ago."

"I think of Christmas and remember your family, Tony. I always thought they had such a wonderful way of celebrating—all the cooking and preparations and the fun they always had with the younger children." She shook her head. "I used to envy you your family."

"You envied us? That's funny, with your background."

"Everything was always so formal at our home. The traditional tree and trimmings, the carefully wrapped gifts for Tom and me. The formal meal. There was never any laughter, any surprises. We seemed to go through the motions without experiencing any of the feelings of Christmas."

"And what feelings were those?"

She sighed, and her expression became wistful. "The love, the laughter, the sharing, the giving. All the wonderful things that your family seems to take for granted."

He shook his head. "Never for granted. We've always known what we had. I suppose I never realized before that you could see and appreciate all that we shared." He studied her for a moment, then asked, "When did you arrive in town?"

"Last night."

He glanced around the busy mall. "And now you're trying to get your shopping done, I take it?"

She shook her head. "Actually, I've already done that back in Boston. No, I just wanted to get out of the house today."

"How is your mother these days?" he asked politely, ignoring the undercurrent between them.

"Busy, as usual. She's so pleased that I decided to come to Portland for Christmas. She and Tom have always flown East each year, since my father died."

"I'm sure your brother was just as pleased that you came home."

"I suppose. Tom and I don't talk much."

"I see."

There were so many questions she wanted to ask him, so many things she wanted to know. But how could she? It was none of her business. Tony D'Angelo was no longer a part of her life. It was obvious that he had accepted that. Natalie had thought she had accepted it years ago. And she had. Of course she had. But only when she had the entire continent between them.

"How long are you going to be here?" he was asking her, and she forced herself to concentrate on his question. "I'm leaving the Monday after Christmas."

"Then you won't be here for New Year's."

"No. I have to get back."

How was it possible that they could be carrying on this perfectly normal conversation, like old friends who had been out of touch for a while, as though there was nothing between them?

But of course there *was* nothing between them now. Her father had seen to that—six years ago.

Chapter Two

Look, I've got to go," Natalie said, gathering her purse and packages. "Mother will be wondering about me. I borrowed Tom's car, and he's probably irritated that I've been gone this long."

Tony got to his feet. The smile he gave her didn't quite reach his eyes. "I'm sorry you have to rush off. I was rather hoping to hear about your life since we last saw each other."

She looked up at him, surprised by his interest. "Most of the time I was in school."

He seemed to hesitate. "I'm sure my family would be pleased to see you again. Would you like to come over some evening while you're here? I could pick you up."

Natalie's pulse began to race. Was this actually happening? Did Tony D'Angelo want to see her again, to spend additional time with her, after all that had happened between them?

Was there such a thing as a second chance?

"I'm not at all sure that you're right, Tony. I doubt that they want to see me after all this time."

"You might be surprised. Of course, it's up to you."

"I'd like to see them again, Tony. I'd like that very much."

His slow smile set up a vibration within her that caused her to almost visibly tremble. "Good. When could you go?"

"I really don't have anything planned."

"Then how about tomorrow night? I could pick you up at seven, if that would be convenient."

"That would be fine," she heard herself saying, as though from far away.

They parted, and only after Tony disappeared in the crowd did Natalie face the fact that except for the time when she'd been accidentally knocked into him and when he'd guided her through the crowd, Tony had carefully refrained from touching her.

What was she doing to herself? This was going to be some kind of refined torture, to become a part, once again, of the D'Angelo gathering at Christmastime.

Torture or not, she couldn't resist. How could anyone resist magic?

That night Natalie disgustedly punched her pillow and tried to straighten her rumpled bedclothes. She was tired. Fighting holiday crowds and traffic was always wearing, and she had gone to bed early, hoping to get some rest.

It was no use. Every time she closed her eyes she saw a pair of black eyes watching her. Sometimes their expression was warm and loving. At other times they held no expression at all.

Tony had handled their unexpected meeting today so well, without showing any shock or surprise. Was that an indication of how little his emotions had been affected by their meeting?

Natalie reminded herself that he had been standing at the jewelry counter—the *women's* jewelry counter, which strongly suggested there was definitely a woman in his life.

What else did she expect, anyway? Tony was extremely attractive. He always had been. She smiled, remembering...

She would never forget the summer she first met Tony, when he came to help his family take care of the sloping lawns and gardens of her home. Natalie had counted the days in between.

Not that she got to spend any time with him. That part didn't matter. It was enough for her to be able to watch him as he worked. As the weeks passed, she managed to find out more things about him.

He was the oldest of five children. She discovered that he had three sisters, one of whom, Angela, was Natalie's age, and a brother who was only a few months old. It was plain to Natalie that he loved his family very much.

By the time Natalie started high school she knew that there would never be any man who could possibly take Tony's place in her heart. In six years she had watched him become a man. He'd stopped working at her home after a couple of summers, but Natalie was able to see him occasionally because of Angela.

She had met Angela her first day of high school. The school was large, covering a vast district. As soon as she saw Angela she knew that the girl was related to Tony, with her curly black hair and dark eyes.

Angela had been shy but pleasant. Natalie and she quickly became friends. Although she could never convince Angela that she would be welcome in Natalie's home, eventually Angela had begun to invite Natalie to the D'Angelo home.

Natalie didn't deliberately lie to her mother about her whereabouts. It was true that Natalie was busy with school-related activities. However, there were times when meetings and other activities ended early, and luckily for Natalie the D'Angelos lived close to the school.

Not that she was ashamed of Angela or the D'Angelo family, but Natalie had learned early in life that her family had decided ideas about who she should spend time with. Her father, especially, had set stringent rules about her dating and the young men who he would consider worthy of her attentions.

Because of Natalie's shyness, most of those young men soon lost interest and went in search of more lighthearted friends. Natalie was content to help Angela with her younger sisters and brother. And when Tony happened to come home while she was still there, Natalie's day was complete. She lived for the times when she happened to see him.

Even the fact that he treated her much in the same way he treated Angela made no impression on her. He was Tony, and that was enough. His flashing smile and teasing remarks were cherished like a priceless treasure.

It was the summer between her junior and senior years, when she was seventeen, that everything changed between them.

Natalie had finally coaxed Angela into meeting Natalie's mother. Her mother seemed relieved that the two rather quiet girls had formed a friendship. She had heard enough stories from her friends about some of the wild parties and problems occurring around their children.

Consequently Natalie spent most of her summer at the D'Angelos' home with her mother's silent blessing.

She would never forget the first time that Tony asked her for a date. She and Angela had just come from swimming at Natalie's home. They were late and rushed back to the D'Angelos' because Angela had promised to cook dinner for Tony since the rest of the family had gone out of town for the weekend.

Tony was working full-time in construction, his only means of transportation a rather beat-up motorcycle. They had just gotten home and hadn't had time to change out of their suits when he walked into the house, looking hot and very tired.

"Oh, Tony," Angela wailed, "I'm sorry. The time just slipped away from us. I'll make you something to eat right away."

He sat down at the table. "Don't worry about it, Angie. It's too hot to eat right now, anyway." His gaze slid from his sister to Natalie, who was self-consciously tugging at her suit. Why hadn't she worn the new one she'd purchased the week before? This one was last year's and too small. It hadn't mattered to her when they'd first gotten the idea to get some relief from the unusual heat of the day.

Now she wished she'd taken the time to have searched for the new one instead of standing there wishing she could disappear.

Tony grinned, the mischief in his eyes apparent. "Hi, Natalie. That's a lovely shade of red you're wearing."

She glanced down at her faded blue suit, then looked up, puzzled.

"I'm talking about the color in your cheeks. No doubt you got too much sun today. You'd better be careful with your fair skin."

His eyes seemed to assess the condition of her skin, from her face down to her toes, lingering along the length of her legs.

"Uh, Angela, I'm going to go change clothes. Then I'll help you with dinner."

"I have a better idea," Tony said. "Why don't both of you go change, and I'll take you out for pizza."

"Oh, but Mama said that I was supposed to feed you," Angela replied.

"She won't care, as long as we eat. And it's too hot to cook."

Angela didn't need much coaxing, and the girls scurried to Angela's room.

Natalie could still remember that night. They had laughed and talked. Tony had seemed content to listen to their chatter. He'd subtly questioned Natalie about her activities, her interests and the boys in her life.

Angela had embarrassed her by pointing out that Natalie showed no interest in the boys *at school*. The emphasis was made for Natalie's benefit, and was the closest that Angela would come to letting Tony know where Natalie's affections lay.

It hadn't taken Angela long to discover Natalie's secret crush on her older brother. Since she quickly learned to love Natalie, Angela could think of nothing better than for her to love Tony. Angela worshiped her brother and always had.

But she had been zealous in never alluding to Natalie's feelings for Tony. Until that night.

Natalie retaliated by kicking her under the table, which elicited a spate of giggles from Angela. Tony looked mystified.

And later it was Tony who insisted on taking Natalie home—on the back of his motorcycle. He found her a helmet and made sure that she had a good grip around his waist before they left. Angela's sparkling smile when they drove off was filled with glee.

Natalie had never been that close to Tony before, and she reveled in it. He'd showered before taking them out for dinner, and she could distinguish the slight scent of soap and after-shave. She rested her head against his back and closed her eyes. Natalie didn't care how long the trip took. She could have stayed that way forever.

When they pulled into the driveway, Natalie noted that her parents were gone. Tony followed the driveway to the back, coming to rest near the garage.

After he helped her off, Tony turned as though to get back on the motorcycle again. Natalie found herself saying, "Do you have to go?"

He looked up, surprised.

"I mean, well, it's such a beautiful night and all. Wouldn't you like to sit out here and talk for a while?" She gestured toward the tables and chairs by the pool.

He glanced around. "Where are your parents?"

"They were invited to a dinner party tonight."

"And they left you here alone?"

She laughed. "Hardly. Charles and Harriet live up there." She pointed to the apartment located over the garage. "Charles always waits until my parents are home before making sure the house is locked and going home."

"What does Harriet do?"

"Cooks and does some of the light cleaning."

"Is that why you're always over at our place, learning to cook?"

She nodded, shyly. "Yes. Harriet doesn't like me messing around in her kitchen. Besides," she said with a toss of her head, "she doesn't know how to cook Italian."

Tony stroked one of the loose blond curls that lay on Natalie's shoulders. "And you want to learn how to cook Italian?"

Natalie was thankful that the moonlight concealed her blush. "Yes, I do."

"Why?" he asked bluntly.

She shrugged and glanced around, desperately looking for another topic of conversation. Spying the pool, she blurted out, "Would you like to go swimming?"

He laughed. "Sure. Unfortunately I don't have anything to swim in."

"That's no problem. We have extras." She grabbed his hand. "I'll show you." She led him to the cabana at the end of the pool. Holding up her bag, she said, "I'll slip my suit back on and meet you out here in a few minutes."

Natalie was trembling so, she could scarcely get undressed. Tony was there, and they were going swimming...in the moonlight. It was the most romantic moment she could possibly imagine.

By the time she came out of the dressing room, Tony was already in the water, swimming laps. The moonlight glinted off the water, bathing him in a glow of light as he moved rapidly through the water.

Natalie quickly joined him, and he began to pace her, matching his strokes to hers. When she could not swim another stroke Natalie grabbed the edge and gasped, "I give up! I'm going to drown if I don't stop!" Her breath came in short pants.

Tony laughed. "I'd never let you drown, Natalie. You know that." He placed his hands on the side of the pool, one on each side of her, so that she was boxed in.

Her heart was racing so fast it was almost painful in her chest, and Natalie couldn't seem to get her breath. Tony was no longer smiling. In fact, she had never seen him look at her so seriously.

"You are so beautiful, Natalie, you seem almost unreal to me. Those silvery-blue eyes staring at me so innocently almost unman me completely." His voice was low, and he spoke haltingly, as though the words had been dragged out of him.

"I'm real," she managed to say softly.

He groaned. "Don't I know it." He glanced around. "I don't think this was such a good idea, after all."

"Why not?"

He shook his head. "Come on, let's get dressed."

Tony was only a few inches away from her, and Natalie couldn't resist the temptation to find out what it would be like to kiss Tony D'Angelo.

Before he could pull away, she let go of the side of the pool and placed her hands lightly on his shoulders. Then she leaned over and kissed him very softly on his lips.

She felt his start of surprise, then her body floated against his, touching his bare chest and legs. His mouth opened slightly, and he began to return her kiss without ever letting go of the side of the pool.

Natalie felt safe in the circle of his arms, and she relaxed more fully against him. Tony deepened the kiss, nudging her lips apart with his tongue. Natalie thought she would faint from the joy of sharing this intimate act with him.

When he finally pulled away, they were both breathing hard. Tony grasped her firmly around the waist and lifted her to the side of the pool, then vaulted up beside her. Without saying a word he pulled her into his arms again, this time holding her tightly against him as he repeated the lesson he'd just given her.

Natalie was eager to learn all that he taught, and she wrapped her arms around his neck, luxuriating in the feel of his crisp curls beneath her fingertips.

Tony's hand eventually slipped from her back to her breast. Natalie couldn't conceal her gasp, and Tony abruptly let go of her.

"What am I doing?" he muttered. "I must be insane." He glanced down at her. "I'm sorry, Natalie."

"I'm not," she replied. "I've dreamed of kissing you for years." Then she realized what she'd admitted to him and covered her face with her hands.

"Natalie?" he said in a wondering tone.

She refused to look at him.

"Natalie?" he repeated. "What are you saying? That you want to go out with me, spend time with me? What?"

Slowly she removed her hands from her face and looked at him. "Only if you want to be with me."

He shook his head. "I've spent years reminding myself that you aren't for me, that I shouldn't show my interest in you, and now you're telling me that—"

"You mean you don't think of me as just another sister?"

He almost choked with his laughter. "Hardly."

They stared at each other in silence. Then Tony brought his hand up and rested it against her cheek. She felt the tremor in his fingertips and vaguely recognized the restraint he was placing on himself. "Oh, Natalie. Do you have any idea what you do to me?"

She shook her head.

"I've got to go. Now." He stood up and strode to the dressing room. She sat there and stared at the door that had cut off her view of him until he reappeared. Then she slowly came to her feet. He walked over to her. "Against my own sense of self-preservation, I'm going to call you for a date. I'll borrow Dad's car. We'll go to a movie or something. We'll go someplace where there are people and where I'm not so tempted. But I've got to see you again, Natalie. Do you understand?"

She smiled. "I'm glad."

He ran his hand over her damp curls. "I've got to be out of my mind."

"If so, then I've joined you," she said with a shy smile.

He pulled her to him and gave her a brief, hard kiss, then set her away from him. "Good night," he said, and turned away. The sudden sound of his motorcycle in the quiet night seemed to bring a touch of reality to the fantasy evening. Natalie watched Tony pull away. She stood there until he disappeared down the driveway, then turned away to go upstairs to relive the past few hours.

For the next two and a half months she saw Tony every day. She no longer cared what her mother thought, or her father. When her father made his disapproval of their relationship clear, she ignored him for the first time in her life.

She loved Tony. She had loved him for years. And now she had the opportunity to be with him as much as his work schedule would allow. Natalie refused to think of the future. She wanted to enjoy her time with Tony that summer. In her mind's eye each day spent with him was another pearl of memories that she collected until a beautiful strand of shared moments linked them to each other.

Natalie floated through the summer in her own dreamlike state of contentment, until the end of August when her father announced that she would not be returning to the public high school for her senior year. She would be going back East to a private girls' school.

Chapter Three

Tony D'Angelo lay awake for hours the night he saw Natalie at the mall. He went over each and every word that was spoken, looking for clues to how she felt about him.

The changes in her were not surprising. Six years was a long time. Was it too long for feelings to last? She had loved him at one time, that much he was sure of. But what about now?

She had seemed glad to see him, hadn't she? He wasn't sure how he had appeared to her. He'd been too busy guarding his reaction to the sudden, unexpected sight of her.

After six years, he had given up hope of her returning to Portland. He had known that sooner or later he would have to make the effort to contact her one last time, but he had continued to put off that inevitable meeting for as long as possible.

Now he had no choice. She was back, and he had to talk with her. He owed her some explanation regarding his silence for the past six years. Would she understand? Would she even care?

She hadn't asked him why he hadn't attempted to contact her nor had she given any explanations for her silence. He wasn't sure he was ready to hear that she had long ago dismissed him from her life. But then, what could he expect from her?

Six years was a long time. But he had kept his word to her father, long after the man was gone. Tony considered his word his honor. Her brother, Tom, had kept her family's side of the bargain.

Now was the time to bring their situation to an end and hopefully use it as a new beginning.

Tony turned over and lay on his stomach, his thoughts full of memories.

He would never forget the first time he'd ever laid eyes on Natalie. She'd been a shy little girl who looked like an angel to him, the kind that always sat at the very top of the D'Angelo family Christmas tree. She'd worn her hair long, the golden curls cascading down her back in a saucy ponytail. But it was her eyes that had drawn him to her. Those clear blue eyes that seemed to be the window of her soul, as though she had no secrets to hide. The dark fringe of thick lashes had appeared to be almost artificial with her light hair and fair skin.

Tony knew that he'd fallen in love that very first day, when she'd shyly offered him something to drink and some cookies.

How old had she been then? Ten or so, probably. She'd looked like a little porcelain doll, and he'd wanted to wrap her up and take her home with him, to protect her against all the hard knocks that life had to offer.

He still felt the same way. He just wasn't sure what course to take. Perhaps she only needed protection from him. At least her father had always felt that way. Perhaps he had been right.

Well, now she was back in Portland again, and she had agreed to visit his parents with him the next night. That was a start, anyway. He would just have to play it by ear.

He fell asleep thinking about her clear-eyed gaze smiling at him with love.

"Mama, look who I found out shopping yesterday," Tony said, motioning for Natalie to join him in the hallway of the family home. He had kissed and hugged his mother when she opened the door.

"Natalie! What a surprise! Come in, come in. You must be freezing out there." Serena D'Angelo waved her arms and hurried Tony and Natalie into the other room where a merrily dancing fire in the fireplace added to the warmth of the atmosphere.

"Hello, Mrs. D'Angelo. I hope you don't mind that I came along."

"What nonsense. Of course I don't mind. You have been a part of this family for years. Besides, you know me. I always cook enough to feed a couple dozen people." She turned and hurried out of the room. "Papa, you will never guess who Tony brought home with him!"

They stood and listened to the voices from the other room. "What did I tell you?" Tony asked with a grin.

From her place in the center of the room, Natalie slowly turned, taking in everything. Tears filled her eyes. So much was familiar—the decorations and ornaments, the Nativity scene on the mantel, the gaily decorated fir tree in the corner that she knew the family had found and cut down as part of their traditional Christmas celebration.

And yet, she saw signs of change as well—new drapes, a new sofa and chair. The place looked homey and lived in—in addition to being well loved.

For the first time since she'd arrived in Portland, Natalie felt as though she had finally come home.

"What's wrong?" Tony asked, concerned.

She shook her head. "Nothing. It's just so good to be here. I didn't think I'd ever see any of this again."

He held out his hand. "Let's go find the others. I forgot to ask if Angela and Paul were coming."

Natalie soon found herself accepted into the laughing circle of the family as though she had never been away. The changes were more apparent at the dinner table. There were only two children still living at home, and they had changed so much that Natalie wasn't certain she would have recognized them. Tony's brother was now fourteen and bore a distinct resemblance to the boy she'd met so many years before.

The D'Angelos were such a warm, loving family. She enjoyed watching the banter and teasing that seemed to be a part of their conversation.

At one point, Serena turned to Natalie and said, "I called Angela and told her you were here. She said that Paul was working late tonight but they would try to come over in time to have coffee and dessert with us." She patted Natalie's hand. "Angela was very excited to know you were here. She has lots of news for you."

Natalie had missed Angela. She had never made another friend who had been as close to her as Angela. Natalie felt as though she'd lost so much that was irreplaceable when she moved back East.

She wondered how Angela would treat her now.

"So tell us what you've been doing, Natalie," Serena continued after making certain that everyone had all that they wanted to eat.

Natalie glanced around and saw that the whole family was waiting for her answer.

"Mostly going to school. I've been doing some graduate work, learning how to help children who have learning disabilities."

"Where do you intend to work when you're through with your schooling?" Serena asked.

Natalie shook her head. "I don't know."

"I'm sure you could find something in the Portland area if you wanted," she pointed out.

Natalie's gaze met Tony's intent one. "That's true," she said softly, wondering what would happen if she were to move back to Portland. Two days ago she would never have considered the idea. Now that she had seen Tony again, her mind seemed to be coming up with some rather unusual ideas.

Serena went on. "I know you must be proud of Tony. Hasn't he done well?"

Natalie looked at Tony sitting there so relaxed beside her. His hand rested alongside hers, and she had an almost uncontrollable urge to touch him. "What do you mean?" she asked, reluctantly forcing her attention toward Serena.

"Hasn't he told you?" Serena asked, beaming. "Tony has his own company now."

Natalie looked at him once more. "Your own company? I don't understand."

He shrugged. "Construction is what I know. I've been going to night school, learning the technical information I needed to build. I started remodeling old homes until I got enough capital to buy one. After that it became a matter of selling the remodeled homes and buying more. I've been doing some new construction as well."

"Oh, Tony. That's wonderful."

"I doubt that your father would have been impressed."

His words seemed to echo and reecho around the room. Her father. Yes, her father's influence on her life still lingered. How different things would have been now without his interference.

"Natalie! You're really here!" Natalie glanced up in time to see Angela rushing toward her. "I couldn't believe it when Mama said you had come to visit." She hugged Natalie, then whirled around. "Paul, come meet Natalie."

A tall blond-headed man had followed the diminutive brunette into the room and had stood there watching the reunion with a smile on his face. "Hello, Natalie," he said with a nod. "I'm glad to finally meet you."

Serena motioned to two empty chairs and said, "Sit! Sit! You're just in time for some cake and ice cream."

"Oh, no, Mama, I can't. I'm having to watch everything I eat these days."

Natalie looked at her slim friend in surprise. "Surely you're not dieting, Angie?"

Angela chuckled. "Not exactly. But I'm still having trouble with nausea in the morning, and I've discovered that it's much easier to eat lightly the night before."

Natalie looked from her friend's face to those seated around the table. "Is this news to anyone besides me?"

They all burst out laughing. Serena explained, "Angie insisted that she wanted to be the one to tell you. I thought we managed to stay off the subject very well, didn't you?"

"Oh, Angela. I'm so happy for you." Flashes of previous conversations they had had over the years came back to her. They had both wanted large, happy families. It looked as though Angela was well on the way to starting hers. Natalie felt a flash of envy at her friend's good fortune. She glanced at Tony and found his intent gaze on her. She dropped her eyes, unable to face him.

Once upon a time she and Tony had talked about the family they wanted to have some day. That was another life ago, before she had decided to train to help other people's children.

She looked at Serena. "So you are going to have a grandchild, are you?"

Serena laughed. "Yes. I can hardly wait."

No one mentioned that Tony, being the oldest, had been the most likely candidate to produce the first grandchild. Natalie glanced down at her hands, which restlessly twisted in her lap.

Tony reached down and touched her hands lightly, as though gently soothing her. She looked up at him, startled by the gesture. What she saw in his face made her realize that he, too, remembered their plans.

The conversation continued with numerous interruptions and hilarious anecdotes as each family member shared with Paul some of the situations that Natalie and Angela used to find themselves in while trying to learn to cook.

Natalie couldn't remember the last time she had laughed so hard nor felt so loved and accepted. After clearing the table and cleaning the dishes, the family returned to the living room where Natalie found herself sandwiched on the small sofa between Tony and his younger brother.

Tony had pulled Natalie against his side with his arm around her shoulders as though it were normal and a routine they had established in front of his family. She smiled at the thought. He had always treated her with such careful distance whenever they'd been around the family in the past, making sure that they understood he was taking no liberties with her.

Now he seemed to be making a silent claim on her, one that was deeply affecting her. How had she possibly stayed away from him this long without making some effort to know if what they had once shared was salvageable? Because if it was—if his body language this evening was any indication—Natalie knew that God in His mercy was willing to give her another chance at happiness.

"Are you ready to go?" Tony asked Natalie some time later, after Angela mentioned that she needed to get home and get some rest.

Natalie smiled. "I'm never ready to leave this place," she said, coming to her feet and hugging Serena. "But I do need to get home. It's been so wonderful, seeing everyone again and sharing one of your marvelous meals. Thank you so much for dinner."

"You're quite welcome," Serena replied, hugging her back. "What are you planning to do for Christmas, Natalie?"

"We haven't discussed anything, actually. My brother's tied up in some big business negotiations and is seldom home. Mother's been busy with Christmas plans for some of the organizations she works with, but she hasn't said anything about our family plans."

"Well, you're welcome to come over here. You know we still have the open house on Christmas Eve, and we all go to the church services at midnight." Serena glanced at her oldest son. "You were planning to come, weren't you, Tony?"

"Of course, Mama. I've never missed spending Christmas with you, now have I?" he said, giving her a hug.

One of the many things that Natalie had always admired was the freedom the D'Angelo family had with each other to express their affection. She had never seen her father, or even her brother, hug her mother. She couldn't remember the last time either her mother or brother had touched her.

There was so much she missed about this family. Watching Tony she knew that she would give everything she owned to be a part of it now.

Tony was quiet during the drive to Natalie's former home located in the west hills overlooking Portland. Natalie wanted to say something, anything to break the silence.

"I take it you're no longer living at home," she finally said.

Tony glanced at her, then returned his gaze to the road in front of them. "No. I'm living in one of the houses I'm currently remodeling."

"Would it be possible for me to see it?" she asked. "Now?"

Her heart seemed to be thundering in her chest. What did he think she meant? She wasn't sure, herself. She'd just been trying to fill in some of the silence between them, trying to overcome the tension that had appeared as soon as they were alone.

"I don't think that would be a very good idea," she said, knowing that she was admitting a great deal more than she'd wanted to by her statement.

Tony didn't reply but continued toward her home.

They pulled into the long driveway that followed the hillside up to the large home. Instead of parking in front, Tony continued around to the back entrance. He turned off the lights and engine of the car, then turned to her. "If you really want to see my place, I could take you over there after I finish working tomorrow."

The light over the garage created shadows across his face, and she couldn't read his expression. "I'd like that," she admitted softly.

Tony looked at the garage, the house, the swimming pool, then back at her. "This feels very familiar, doesn't it? Bringing you home like this? Wondering if we woke up your parents?"

She smiled. "You have to admit that this car is considerably different from your old pickup or the motorcycle."

He grinned. "True. I doubt that anyone in the neighborhood heard us drive in this time."

They stared at each other in silence. Tony placed his hand on her cheek and gently brushed his thumb across her slightly parted lips. "I've missed you," he finally said in a husky voice.

"I missed you, too. I guess I just assumed that you never wanted to see me again."

He stroked along her ear and down her neck as though relearning the shape and feel of her. "Why would you think that?"

"Because of what happened. Because I never heard from you after I left."

He tilted her chin so that she had no other option but to look at him, unless she closed her eyes. She was tempted by the thought—to close her eyes and move the necessary few inches to kiss Tony again, to experience the wonderful magic that only he seemed to evoke. But she had to know. Why hadn't he tried to contact her through the years? She had asked Angela to have him write to her, but she hadn't heard from either of them.

He leaned over and placed a gentle kiss at her temple, his touch feeling like butterfly wings brushing against her sensitive skin.

"I couldn't contact you. That was part of the agreement."

She stared up at him in confusion. "What agreement?"

"The one I made with your father."

"I don't know what you're talking about."

"I'm not surprised."

"He told you to leave me alone?"

"What else did you expect from him? He never accepted me in your life. He made his disapproval very obvious, particularly that last time I saw you."

She could feel the heat rising to her face, but could not control it. How many years had she tried to forget that last time she'd been with Tony? She shook her head. "I was so frightened."

"I know. I even understood your reaction at the time. But it still hurt."

She placed her hand on his arm. "I never wanted to hurt you, Tony. Please believe me."

"I know. I understood that at the time. You were very young. You were faced with a decision you weren't prepared to make."

"You're right. I thought I'd made all the decisions that were necessary." She could feel her heart racing in her chest. She wanted him to kiss her and hold her, to reassure her that his feelings hadn't changed for her. If he were to ask her to stay in Portland, she would willingly do so. But how could she understand how he felt if he didn't say anything?

He leaned over and lightly kissed her on the lips, then pulled away from her. "I'd better get you inside. It's late."

Natalie tried to hide her reaction, hoping that the shadows masked her expression. What had she expected, anyway? They were both too old to sit out in the car like a couple of teenagers.

"Why don't I come by tomorrow early enough to show you the house before dark? Then we can have dinner together somewhere."

She smiled. "I'll be ready whenever you say." Tony got out of the car and walked around to her side. She waited until he had opened her door, then said, "I want you to know how much I appreciated getting to see your family tonight. Being with them brought back so many happy memories."

"Yes, it did. We used to enjoy teasing you and Angela so much. I'd almost forgotten."

They reached the screened porch and paused. The cold night air seemed to move around them in swirls. "Sleep well," he said with a smile, holding the door open for her. "I'll see you tomorrow."

Natalie nodded. "You do the same," she said, and hurried inside to the warmth of the house.

Natalie slowly climbed the stairway to her room. Memories of her last Christmas in Portland continued to stir around her, as though insisting on being recalled and acknowledged.

After going through her nightly ritual of getting ready for sleep, Natalie stretched out on the bed and pulled the covers up around her.

If only she could understand the man that Tony had become. He acted so natural around her, as though he were comfortable with her. Was she the only one feeling the tension that seemed to hold her prisoner whenever he was present?

What had happened to the young man she had known, the one she had fallen so much in love with? Did he still exist somewhere beneath that calm and controlled exterior?

The hovering memories swooped down around her, eager to gain her attention once again.

Chapter Four

After almost four months away from home, Natalie still hated the boarding school. She missed Angela and her friends at school. But most of all, she missed Tony. After having seen him every day during the summer, the sudden jolt of being away from him had been almost more than she could handle. Her father had not even allowed her to come home for Thanksgiving, insisting she take the time to get better acquainted with her new classmates before coming home for Christmas.

With only another week before Christmas, Natalie hurriedly packed so that she would be ready to catch her ride to the airport. She felt like she'd been away from home for years instead of months.

She'd written Tony almost every day that she'd been gone. He had managed to respond to a few of her letters, admitting that he wasn't very good at corresponding, but that didn't mean that he wasn't counting the days until she arrived home for Christmas vacation.

Natalie had kept a large calendar hanging over her desk and had drawn a large X through each day before going to bed. At long last she would be able to see him again, even though she wasn't sure how.

Her father had refused to be swayed from his decision to send her away last September. She had cried. She had pleaded. Never in her life had Natalie wanted so desperately to stay home, but he would not relent.

He made it clear that his daughter was going to have a proper education and meet the right kind of people. Her summer rebellion was now over.

She hadn't even been given the opportunity to tell Tony goodbye. Instead, she'd had to send a message through Angela.

Natalie had learned a great deal in the past few months. She had learned not to be so open and trusting. She had always thought that her parents respected her, including her beliefs and opinions. She had learned that she was wrong. She would never make that mistake again.

Natalie had no intention of telling her family that she was going to spend any time with the D'Angelos. She had made sure that her letters were full of the new people she'd met and all of her activities. As far as her parents knew, she had forgotten her old friends.

By the time she'd been home for two days, she could tell that she had convinced them of her lack of interest in anyone in Portland. She made a great many remarks about how boring it was to be home and how she could hardly wait to return East. Watching the satisfied glance her father gave her mother convinced Natalie that she could have a career in acting if she chose. She had managed to cover her true feelings.

Consequently she was given a great deal of freedom to come and go as she pleased, which suited her just fine. She spent every available minute at the D'Angelo home.

Tony was the one who wasn't pleased when she refused to allow him to take her home. He was much harder to convince that what she was doing was the only way she could still see him without creating all sorts of difficulties with her family.

They even argued about it.

"Don't you see, Tony? This is the only way I can see you!"

"Don't give me that! We aren't in the Dark Ages, you know. You're eighteen years old, Natalie. Your father has no say-so over you."

She nodded. "But he does. I'm still in school."

"So what?"

"I have no choice but to go by his rules as long as he's taking care of me."

"Then let me take care of you."

They were in his car at a secluded lookout near the Columbia River, and she looked at his shadowed face in surprise. "What do you mean?"

"Marry me, Natalie. I can take care of you. Then you can go to school here. We have the community college and Portland State if you want to go further. Just don't go back East."

"Oh, Tony," she whispered, her heart seeming to pound in her throat. "Do you really mean that?"

He pulled her into his arms. "Of course, I mean it. I can support you. I love you. I want to marry you. I can't stand the thought of your being so far away."

His kiss made it clear to her that he wanted her in every way that a man could want a woman. Natalie surrendered to his touch, trembling in his arms. When he drew away, they were both having trouble breathing.

She shook her head. "You know they'd never allow that," she managed to say.

"They can't stop us."

"What do you mean?"

He nodded to the other side of the river. "We could go over to Washington and get married. They wouldn't have to know anything about it until it was already accomplished."

"Are you serious?"

The kiss he gave her removed any doubt in her mind. When he finally raised his head, his voice was husky with longing. "I've never wanted anything more in my life."

"But what will they do when they find out?"

"What can they do? They'll just have to accept the fact that we're married." He brushed a stray curl away from her brow. "It's the only way I know to keep them from sending you back East after the holidays."

The thought of being married to Tony D'Angelo caused Natalie's heart to triple its rhythm. To actually be married to him, to live with him, sleep with him, have his children was more than she'd ever envisioned.

She couldn't think of anything she'd rather have happen in her life. "All right," she managed to say, her voice quavering.

This time it was Tony who needed reassurance. "Do you really mean it, Natalie?" She nodded her head, and he hugged her to him. "You'll never regret it, Natalie. I promise. I'll make you happy, I swear."

She laughed. "You don't have to do anything to make me happy, Tony. Being with you is all that it takes."

He stroked her cheek. "I love you so much, Natalie. I can't begin to tell you how much."

"I love you, too."

He shook his head. "But you're so young. Maybe we should wait awhile. Maybe until after you've graduated."

She pulled away from him. "You want me to spend five more months away from you?"

He shook his head. "No."

She grinned. "So what do we have to do?"

He was silent for several minutes. "Tomorrow is Christmas Eve. We always have an open house and go to midnight services. Are you going to be able to come?"

"I think so. My parents are having some people in, and I told them I'd be going to church. They probably won't know when I leave."

"If you could get away early, say around noon, we can go to Vancouver, get a license and find a judge to marry us. Then we'll spend the evening with my parents. Instead of taking you home, we'll go to a hotel. I'll take you home Christmas morning, and we'll tell your family."

"When will we tell yours?"

"Not until after we've told your family. We'll go back home and spend Christmas with my folks."

"Your family is going to be hurt at our doing it this way."

Tony was quiet for a moment. "I know. And you won't be having the kind of wedding that you and Angie have always talked about, I'm afraid."

"I don't care," she said, tracing his jawline with her finger. "All I care about is being with you." Her voice broke. "I can't stand being away from you, Tony."

"Then this is the only way I know to keep you here." He held her so close that she could feel his heart beating, its rapid rhythm telling her better than words how she affected him.

Tony had been so careful with her ever since he'd first started seeing her. She had been aware of the tight rein he'd kept on his reactions to her, but she wasn't so naive that she hadn't understood what a strain he'd been under.

By this time tomorrow night, they would be married. He wouldn't have to keep such a rigid control over his actions.

The next day there was talk of snow for Christmas, and her mother warned her about driving in the bad weather. Natalie laughed at the idea. She wouldn't be going far. She explained that she had some last minute errands to run and some gifts to deliver and that she wasn't sure when she'd be home.

She met Tony at noon.

They were in the clerk's office in Vancouver by one o'clock and by two had found a benevolent judge who agreed to marry them.

By two-thirty they were back in Portland. Natalie couldn't believe it. She was actually married to Tony.

She was now Natalie Phillips D'Angelo, and she had the ring to prove it. "It's beautiful, Tony," she said, touching the wide gold band on her third finger.

"Not as beautiful as you. Someday in the near future I'm going to buy you an engagement ring to go with it."

"I don't need one, Tony. This is all I need."

He took her hand and placed it on his thigh. "I wasn't sure you'd be there today."

"Why?"

"I thought you might have second thoughts about the idea."

"All I could do was to count the hours."

"Where did you tell your mother you were going?"

"I had some last-minute shopping. If I go home now, she won't think anything of my leaving later."

"I'm not sure I can let you leave me, even for a few hours," he said, pulling up beside her car in the parking lot where she'd left it earlier.

She threw her arms around him. "This will be the last time. I promise."

He hugged her tightly against him. "I'll see you at our place this evening."

"Yes."

"I love you, Natalie."

Those words echoed in Natalie's mind all that afternoon. She hurried home and helped her mother prepare for their guests. She made sure the gifts she'd brought from school were under the tree so that her parents and brother would find them the next morning.

For just a moment she had a strong desire to tell them about her marriage, but Tony had cautioned her against that. He wanted to be with her when they heard the news.

Besides, she wanted this particular night with Tony before they told anyone. For a little while they would share their special secret only between the two of them.

By the time she quietly left the house, her parents' guests had begun to arrive. She had no difficulty in slipping outside with her overnight case.

The sky had cleared, and the twinkling lights from downtown Portland were no competition to the bright stars that seemed to be specially polished for this particular night.

Natalie drove slowly through the streets, enjoying the many decorated homes. The crisp air seemed to shimmer with the echoes of church bells and carols being sung.

Such a special night. One that she would never forget. She and Tony had picked a beautiful time to be married, to share the love they felt for each other with the love that had been brought to the Earth almost two thousand years before.

Tony met her at the door of his parents' home, giving her a brief, possessive kiss before escorting her into the room filled by members of their family and a collection of laughing friends.

"I missed you," he whispered. "Are you sure you want to stay here all evening?" He couldn't hide the desire in his eyes.

"Don't you think we should?"

"Yes. But I don't know how much longer I can be around you without shouting to the world that you now belong to me."

She hugged him tightly, thrilled at the leashed control he was keeping on his emotions. When he finally let go, she would be able to show him how much she loved and wanted him as well.

"None of that, you two," Angela warned with a grin. She was carrying a large tray of food to the buffet table set up near the Christmas tree. "You don't want to be shocking anyone with your behavior now, big brother."

Tony grinned, refusing to remove his arms from around Natalie.

The rest of the evening passed in a blur to Natalie. When it was time to leave for church, she and Tony managed to slip away in his car without offering to take anyone with them. They didn't intend to return to the house. Natalie had placed her bag in his car when she arrived.

The church bells were ringing as family clusters went through the front doors of the church. Once inside each person was handed a candle.

The service, as always, touched Natalie's heart. After the story of the Nativity was read aloud, the lights in the church were dimmed and each candle was lit. The smiles around her were so beautiful. The shared love was so tangible that Natalie felt that she could reach out and almost touch it.

She was so glad to spend this time with Tony, to be reminded of the magic of Christmas, that time of year when people took time out of their busy lives to remember the wonderful gift they had been given, the example they had been shown on how to love one another. It was a gift that could be carried with them throughout the new year.

After the service Tony quietly took her hand and led her out of the church. Silently they walked to the car and drove to one of the luxury hotels downtown that overlooked the Willamette River.

He carried their small cases and went inside. Without pausing at the desk he walked over to the elevator.

"Don't we have to register?"

He glanced down at her. "I checked in earlier."

"Oh."

When he opened the door to the room, Natalie walked in and stopped, awed by the view.

The moonlight shone brightly over the city and highlighted the snow that coated Mount Hood in a pristine white blanket.

"I left the drapes open. I thought you might appreciate the view."

"It's beautiful, Tony," she murmured, moving over to the window and staring outside. The lights along the many bridges spanning the river were reflected in the water, so that the entire city seemed to be a gigantic ornament lit up for their pleasure.

Tony pulled her against him, her back resting against his chest. "I hoped you would like it."

She turned in his arms. "Thank you. Thank you for being who you are, for being so thoughtful and considerate. Thank you for loving me."

"You don't owe me any thanks, love. I got to marry the Christmas-tree angel. What more could any mortal ask?"

His kiss was gentle, as though he didn't want to frighten her. At last, after all these months together, there were no more restrictions between them.

Natalie felt so loved and protected. She had loved this man since they had both been children. Now they were grown. Now they were married.

Now they belonged to each other.

Tony dropped his arms and stepped back. "I don't want to rush you. I want this night to be special."

"It already is."

He nodded to the bathroom where the only light they had glowed. "You can change in there if you'd like."

She could feel herself blushing, despite everything she could do. Why should she feel shy with Tony? She loved him. She wanted him to show her how to express that love physically.

Somehow he must have known how she felt. He touched her cheek softly and smiled. Turning away, she opened her case and pulled out her gown and robe. "I'll only be a few minutes," she whispered, picking up her bag of toiletries.

"There's no rush. We have the rest of our lives together."

When she came out, she turned off the bathroom light. Moonlight poured through the large expanse of glass, illuminating the room so that she could see Tony was already in bed, waiting for her.

Natalie moved silently toward him. She let the robe slide from her shoulders and fall to the floor beside the bed. Then she shyly slid under the covers beside him.

Tony turned onto his side and leaned on his elbow. "You are so beautiful, I'm afraid to touch you for fear you're not real."

She rested her hand on his bare chest. "I'm real enough." She could feel the heat of his skin almost burning her fingertips.

He touched her hair lightly, brushing it out over the pillowcase. Then he traced the shape of her ear with his forefinger.

Natalie turned her head so that she could see him. His dark eyes glittered in the moonlight, and she could see the tension in his face.

For the first time, Natalie realized that he was as nervous as she was. Recognizing that fact helped her to relax. She tilted her head so that she could kiss him.

His mouth felt so familiar, so dear to her. She remembered the months that she had lain awake at night, wishing he were there to kiss her good-night. Now her dreams had come true on this most magical of all nights. Tony was there to share his love with her.

As the kiss continued, the soft gentleness began to change. It became heated, moist and more demanding. Natalie felt as though she were igniting. Everywhere he touched, Tony's caressing hands seemed to set off tiny explosions of excitement within her.

He began to explore her face with his kisses while his hands followed the contours of her body. Although he had never taken such liberties before, Natalie felt no qualms about allowing the intimacies. This was Tony, and he was turning her into an inferno.

She could no longer lie still and restlessly began to trace the well-developed muscles of his shoulders and back.

When his kisses moved down along the low neckline of her gown, Natalie shivered. He raised his head and looked at her. "Did I hurt you?"

She shook her head. His hand cupped her breast. "Would you rather I not touch you?"

"I love you to touch me, Tony."

He slid his hand under first one strap, then the other, then slowly pushed the gown down until it was around her waist.

Natalie had always been shy, and yet she loved the expression that Tony had on his face when he looked at her. When he leaned over and kissed the rose-tipped surface of her breast, she almost cried out with the pleasure of his touch.

She ran her hands restlessly across his chest, then around his back and up through his hair. The curls clung to her fingers as though returning her soft caress.

Natalie clung to him as he worshiped her body. By the time he moved so that he was lying between her legs, she was almost whimpering with longing without understanding what it was she needed.

He showed her—with infinite gentleness he showed her the beautiful ecstasy that two people can share. With patience he allowed her to adjust to him before he began the age old rhythm that brought them ever closer to each other and to the pinnacle of sensation.

His murmured love words filled her mind and heart. She clung to him as though he were the only thing that prevented her from being swept away with all the new sensations. He waited for her to respond, to ignite, to take the lead in finding their goal.

His patience was rewarded. When she gasped, he felt the contractions begin deep within her and could no longer postpone his own reaction. With a soft cry he gave a convulsive lunge and held her as though he never intended to let her go.

"Oh, Tony," she whispered when she could get her breath. "I never knew it could be like this. I never guessed making love would be so wonderful. How could we have waited so long?"

He had rolled to his side, holding her tightly against him. "I had to wait, love. I could never have loved you so intimately, then walked away from you. I had to know you were mine to hold all night, every night."

She smiled, kissing him. "If only I'd known."

"I'm glad you didn't. You were enough of a temptation as it was."

They lay there, sharing memories of the separation they had just gone through, planning for their future, talking about their family. He had been careful to protect her from pregnancy, and they had discussed the need for waiting until she was through with school before starting a family.

Then they had made love once again. This time they took their time—the urgency was gone. There was time for exploration and experimentation. Natalie was eager to learn all about him and what affected him.

When they finally fell asleep it was almost dawn, and they were exhausted.

Which was why they did not hear the key in the lock or the door being opened the next morning.

The first thing they heard was the sound of Natalie's father demanding that they get up, get dressed and get ready to leave.

Chapter Five

With a sob Natalie came awake, shaking. She sat there for a moment, trying to get her breath. She'd been dreaming again, the same dream that had haunted her for years. Why did her subconscious persist in reminding her of the past when she'd worked so hard to forget it?

Instead, she continually relived the nightmarish feeling of waking from a sound sleep to find her father yelling at her and Tony, calling them names she'd never heard coming from her father.

She could still remember the horror of that moment as she scrambled to find the robe she'd discarded the night before beside the bed. She could still hear her father's angry words, threatening Tony.

She had tried to explain that they were married, that they had done nothing wrong, but instead of appeasing him, her explanations called forth an even louder denunciation, most of it aimed at Tony.

Her father had reminded Tony of her youth, her lack of education, her family's plans for her. Then he told them that he intended to have the marriage annulled and that if either one of them gave him any trouble over it, he would see that not only Tony but his entire family would never be able to find work in the entire Pacific Northwest.

Then he'd demanded that Natalie get dressed and come home with him, that her brother was waiting downstairs.

Her humiliation was complete. She felt like a rebellious runaway as she ran into the bathroom to get dressed. She could still hear her father's voice as he continued to roar at Tony. She could hear Tony's attempts to break into the tirade, but without success.

When she had replaced the clothes she'd worn the day before, Natalie had reentered the bedroom. The first thing she noticed was that Tony was up. He wore the pants he'd had on the day before, but was still barefoot and without a shirt. In the bright morning light streaming through the window he looked like a marble statue that could be found in Rome. She was forcibly reminded of the night they had just shared, the intimacies, the passion, and she found herself moving toward him.

"Leave him alone!" her father ordered. "Go on downstairs and wait for me, Natalie."

Tony's calm gaze met hers. "You don't have to leave, Natalie. There's nothing he can do to us, you know."

"The hell there isn't!" her father interrupted to say. "You don't know what trouble is, young man, until you've tangled with me. I've got enough clout in this area to see that you and your father are hounded out, forced to move clear across the country. I'm telling you to leave my daughter alone!"

Tony continued to watch Natalie, waiting for her response.

All she could think about was what her father was saying. It was true. She had seen what he could do. She knew how he had destroyed competitors. What could he do to the D'Angelos if he really set about bringing them down? It didn't bear thinking about.

"Tony?" she whispered, uncertainly.

"Don't go, Natalie. He can't hurt us. You belong to me now!"

Her father blew up with that remark, shouting words that made Natalie cringe. Tony didn't understand. He didn't know the kind of man that her father was capable of being.

But Natalie did. How could she do something that would hurt not only the man she loved but his wonderful loving family as well?

She began to cry. "Oh, Tony."

Tony started toward her, but her father blocked his way.

"Go downstairs, Natalie. Now!" her father said. He looked as though he were ready to strike Tony. "I want you out of her life, D'Angelo. Do you understand? Completely and totally out of her life. I don't care what sort of ceremony you think you went through, there is no marriage. I'll see to that!" He turned to Natalie. "Now get out of here."

Years later, Natalie could still feel the awful pain in her chest. She remembered starting to the door and looking back. The anguish in Tony's eyes was unmistakable. His murmured, "Don't go, Natalie," as she slowly went out of the room continued to haunt her all these years.

She had never seen him again. Not until two days ago when she'd recognized him at the mall.

Her father and brother had driven her home. She'd been hysterical. Her father had told her to forget about Tony and any marriage. The marriage was no longer in existence, he would see to that.

He had sent her back to school the day after Christmas. She had never talked to him again. Three months later her father had had a sudden heart attack and died before they could get him to the hospital.

She had flown home for the funeral, but hadn't attempted to contact Tony or his family. After three months of silence in response to her letters, she had gotten her answer from the D'Angelos. None of them wanted anything more to do with her.

Now, here she was, six years later, back in their lives. They had all been kind to her, including Tony. He had treated the past as though it had never happened, as though they had never spent that marvelous night together, as though he hadn't taught her so much about his own sexuality and hers.

She had stayed in the East once she finished school for the year, taking summer courses and planning her college curriculum. It was as though she could bury herself in a heavy schedule so that she wouldn't have time to think about what she had given up.

Natalie knew that she was responsible for the present situation. The choice had been hers, and she'd made it. If she had it to do over again, she would probably have done the same thing. Even with her father gone, it was too late to go back and attempt to make amends.

She knew that walking out on Tony at that vulnerable time in their relationship had been a betrayal of all that they had shared.

Now he was treating her like a friend. He was relaxed and easy around her. And it was slowly killing her. When she had attempted to discuss what had happened, he had excused what she had done as though it were no longer important.

She glanced at her bedside clock. It was almost four o'clock in the morning. He was coming by later that day to take her to see his home. What did it mean? Why was he willing to spend time with her without discussing anything personal between them? Natalie wondered how she could possibly continue to be around him without betraying her feelings.

She felt as though the past six years had been wiped away and she was once more the eighteen-year-old girl whose bones seemed to melt whenever he appeared.

Some things never change.

When Tony arrived to pick her up, both Tom and her mother were there. Natalie brought him into the living room with her.

"Mother, Tom, I believe you remember Tony D'Angelo, don't you?"

Natalie was surprised to see Tom promptly get up and stride over to Tony. "Hello, Tony. It's good to see you. It's been a while," he said with a smile.

Tony nodded. "I've been busy."

"So I understand. I read in the paper that your company won the bid on the Crandall property."

"That's right."

"Congratulations. Your growth in the industry has been phenomenal."

Natalie could scarcely believe her ears. Tom was talking to Tony as though they were old friends, although Tony was much more reserved. And it was obvious that Tom had been keeping tabs on Tony's company. Why?

"Hello, Tony," her mother said quietly. "How is your family?"

"Doing very well."

"Would you like to join us? We've been having coffee in front of the fire and enjoying a quiet moment. We don't seem to have many of them these days."

He smiled at the older woman. "Not today. I promised Natalie I would take her over to see my latest project, then we're having dinner."

"Yes, she told me. I know she's enjoyed seeing her old friends after such a long absence."

Tony glanced at Natalie from the corner of his eye. "I've enjoyed seeing her as well," he offered in a noncommittal tone.

After Natalie put on her coat, they left the house and walked down the steps to the curving driveway where his late-model sports car waited.

"Quite a different reception than I'm used to from your family," he pointed out quietly after they'd started down the driveway.

"I don't think either my mother or brother shared my father's animosity toward you, Tony."

"So I noticed."

"Tom seemed to be very interested in you."

She noticed that he hesitated a moment before answering her. "Yes, well, we've run into each other occasionally over the years."

"He's never mentioned you whenever we talked."

"There was no reason for him to, was there?"

She shook her head, trying to pull her thoughts away from the past.

She noted that Tony was headed south along the Willamette River, toward Lake Oswego. After several turns and winding streets he pulled into a driveway that was marked Private. They followed it through the dense trees until the driveway split, forming a circle in front of a large home.

Natalie looked at the two-story structure, then back at Tony. "This is where you're living?"

He nodded. "It had been neglected for several years and needed some major renovation. I decided it was worth saving. I've finished up most of the inside work. Now all that needs to be done is cosmetic repair to the outside."

Natalie slowly got out of the car and walked to the door. "This is beautiful, Tony."

And it was. It looked like an English country home, with weathered red bricks and large windows with small panes of leaded glass. She could almost feel the warmth that seemed to radiate from the place.

"The house had been tied up in probate proceedings for years with no one taking proper care of it."

"It has such a happy feel about it, as though you can almost hear the laughter of children," she said as he opened the door into the wide foyer.

He pointed to the curving staircase. "I'm certain that more than one person slid down that railing, aren't you?"

"It certainly is tempting, isn't it?" she said with a grin, running her hands over the smooth-grained surface.

Each room was open. Tony had done an excellent job of lightening the look of the place, painting pastel colors on the walls and refinishing the hardwood floors.

When they walked into the breakfast room, Natalie paused, touched by the view from the multipaned windows. A garden sloped down to the edge of the lake. The profusion of rhododendrons, azaleas and rosebushes told her that the spring and summer would be filled with riotous colors. An arched trellis indicated climbing roses made their home there during the blooming season.

"Oh, Tony," she whispered, enchanted.

"Do you like it?"

"I love it. I've never seen a more homey, comfortable place."

He took her hand and led her through the kitchen that had been thoroughly modernized, then back into the hallway. "Let me show you upstairs."

The upstairs contained four large bedrooms. The master suite had a built-in bath and dressing area that had been completely modernized.

The furniture in the room was distinctively masculine, but not heavy. She caught herself staring at the massive bed that was located on a dais. How many women had shared that bed with Tony? Of course she didn't want to know. It was no longer any of her business. She had walked out of his life.

She turned away, trying to cover her reaction to the room. "This is marvelous, Tony. You've done a wonderful job. Do you intend to put it on the market now that you've completed most of the work?"

"I'm not sure at this point what I intend to do."

"I see."

She wished she did. Tony had not mentioned another woman in his life, and yet she knew that he was entirely too attractive not to have someone. She had listened carefully to his family's conversation, hoping a name would be dropped in the conversation that would give her a clue to his personal life.

If she were more brave, she could question him, but she knew it was none of her business, and she wasn't sure she would be able to handle his answer when she heard it.

"Are you ready to go? I have reservations at one of the restaurants overlooking the river."

She nodded and started toward the door.

"Natalie?"

She turned. He still stood there in the middle of the bedroom, watching her.

"Yes?"

"Do you think I should keep this place?"

She attempted a casual shrug. "I can't really say, Tony. It seems to be a rather large home for one person to occupy."

"I don't intend to live here alone."

A lump seemed to form in her throat, and she had trouble swallowing. "Then you need to ask the woman you intend to share it with."

He was by her side in a few long strides. Gripping her forearms he gave her an intense look. "I'm asking *you*."

Before she could form any words, he pulled her up against him and kissed her, a long, slow, mind-drugging kiss that took her far back into the past to other times, other kisses and to the one unforgettable night they had spent together.

Her arms curled up around his neck, holding him close. She had never forgotten the feel of Tony's arms around her, his powerful body molded tightly against hers. His kiss revealed that the restraint he'd shown around her was merely a facade, and Natalie reveled in the knowledge that she could still affect him so strongly.

When he finally raised his head, his face was flushed and his eyes glittered.

"Let's get out of here now," he muttered, "or I'll never be able to let you walk out of here."

Without looking at it, Natalie was aware of the presence of the large bed waiting only a few feet away. It would be so easy to let him know how much she wanted him again, after all this time.

But giving in to her feelings wouldn't solve anything. After a few hours with Tony in bed, she would once again be faced with a life without him. She didn't need the reminder.

They walked out to the car in silence. When Tony slid behind the steering wheel beside her, she glanced at him and smiled. "You're wearing more lipstick than I am at the moment," she said, handing him her handkerchief.

He glanced in the rearview mirror, then took her handkerchief and slowly removed the color from around his mouth.

"I'm sorry. I didn't mean to do that," he said without looking at her. He returned the handkerchief and started the car.

Natalie decided to be honest. "I'm not. I've wanted to kiss you like that since I saw you the other day in the mall."

He glanced down at her in surprise, then a smile slowly spread across his mouth. "No kidding?"

"No kidding."

He began to laugh. "And here I've been trying to be so careful with you."

"Why?"

"I didn't want to scare you away."

"Tony, there is nothing you can do that would scare me away."

She watched his reaction to her statement. He reflected on it for several moments in silence. Then he spoke. "We need to talk."

"Yes."

"But not tonight. I wanted a quiet evening with you, a chance to get reacquainted." He paused, as though searching for words. "Tomorrow is Christmas Eve."

She knew that they were both remembering what that day meant, but she could find no words to express what she was feeling.

"Natalie, would you spend tomorrow evening with me? We could go to my parents' open house and to church. . . ." He paused, as though unsure of himself.

"I'd like that."

"Would you come back to the house with me, afterward?"

Her heart felt as though it was going to rocket out of her chest at his words.

"We need to talk. There's so much to say, but I'd rather wait until we have enough time and privacy."

He waited, and Natalie knew that a great deal rested on her response. "Yes, Tony. I'll spend as much time with you as you'd like me to."

They both knew what she was agreeing to without further words. He took his hand from the steering wheel and without looking at her, brushed his knuckles gently against her cheek. "Thank you."

How could he possibly be thanking her for agreeing to something she wanted so badly? She was the one who had walked out on him.

When they arrived at the restaurant they were immediately shown to their table. She had never been there before but was impressed with the decor and the privacy afforded each table. They were seated near a wide expanse of glass so that they could see the river and a nearby bridge. A fat candle in an oval glass holder flickered on the table, casting a warm light that created a halo effect to enfold them.

After they had ordered, Tony took her hand in both of his. Looking deep into her eyes, he said softly, "Tell me about you, Natalie. About school, about your friends, your hobbies. Help me learn about the woman that has grown from the young girl I once knew."

Haltingly at first, Natalie described her life. Tony quietly asked probing questions that she answered easily. Her life was open, free of secrets, almost boring.

By the time she had answered all of his questions, they were being offered dessert. She shook her head, sighing. "I couldn't eat another thing." They both ordered coffee, and when the waiter left, she said, "How about you? When are you going to tell me about you?"

"I will. Tomorrow night. I promise." He glanced away for a moment, and once again she was aware of the perfection of his profile. Then his dark eyes met hers once more. "It's getting late, and we both need our rest. I'll pick you up tomorrow to go to the open house."

She nodded, her thoughts flying ahead. Their plans for the next day were so similar to that day six years ago that she had a frightening sense of déjà vu. This time her father wasn't around to make changes in any of their plans. This time Tony was not suggesting marriage. This time she was not a foolish girl with stars in her eyes.

She knew he wanted her, there was no way to miss that. She wanted him, too. If this was all she could have, she was determined that it would be enough.

After all, the Christmas season was once more with them. During that magical time anything could happen. Love could grow and become whole once again.

When Tony took her home he walked her to the front door, refusing her invitation to come in. "They're predicting snow tomorrow. I hope not. There'll be so many people traveling."

"Drive safely," she said, going up on tiptoe and kissing him softly on the mouth. "Take care of you for me."

He grinned. "Always. I'll see you tomorrow."

When she walked inside the house, Tom came out of the living room. "I thought I heard you."

"Where's Mother?"

"She went up to bed. She's tired. Would you like a glass of sherry or wine before going to bed?"

"Sure, why not? Sherry would be nice." She wandered into the living room behind him and walked over to the fireplace. "The fire feels good tonight. I understand there's a chance of snow."

"Yes." He handed her a glass, and she sat down opposite him in one of the chairs in front of the fire. "Did you enjoy dinner?" he asked, watching her.

She nodded.

"Do you intend to spend tomorrow evening with him?"

"Yes, why?"

"I just wondered. You've never talked about Tony to me since you left Portland. I wasn't sure you'd even see him when you came back."

"I probably wouldn't have. We ran into each other accidentally."

"I don't believe in accidents."

"What do you mean? There's no way either of us could have known the other was shopping at the mall that day."

"But you would have seen him, sooner or later." He took a sip of his drink. "I know that you think Dad was very harsh with you and Tony back then."

"'Harsh' isn't the word. He was brutal, and you know it."

"He was concerned about you."

"He had no reason to be."

"Dad loved you very much, Natalie. He wanted what was best for you."

"Except he seemed to think he was the only one who knew best."

Tom shook his head. "Getting married in the middle of your senior year didn't make much sense, did it?"

She looked away from him, watching the fire dancing along the logs. "I loved him. It was the only way we could be together. Besides, I would have gone on with my schooling."

"Unless you had gotten pregnant. There's always that chance."

She shrugged. "What difference does it make now?"

"Do you still love Tony?"

She looked at him, surprised at the personal question. "Of course I love Tony. I always have. I always will. That isn't the issue."

"And what exactly is the issue?"

"Tony has put me out of his mind and life. He doesn't even bring up what happened, as though it means nothing to him."

"Natalie, he's right. You can't continue to live in the past or let the hurts of the past hang around you today. What happened, happened. You can't undo it or change it."

"I know. I really thought I had put it all behind me until I saw him again. I lost so much."

"I don't think 'lost' is the proper word. 'Postponed,' perhaps, would better describe the situation. You're both young yet. You can have so many happy years together, now that he's successfully established in business and you have your education."

"Except for one minor detail."

"What's that?"

"Tony never brings up a future for us. He talks as though we'll both continue on our separate paths."

"He's never suggested that you consider moving back to Portland?"

"Not once."

"Interesting."

"What do you mean?"

"Nothing. I just find Tony D'Angelo an interesting character study." Tom finished his drink and stood. "Then you won't be home tomorrow evening?"

She shook her head. "Not until very late, anyway. I'm not sure what time I'll be home." She couldn't quite meet his eyes. How could she tell her brother that if Tony suggested she spend the remainder of Christmas Eve with him, she would do so, without any qualms?

Natalie set her glass down and got up from the chair. "I'll see you in the morning, Tom. Good night."

His murmured good-night was barely audible as she walked out of the room.

Chapter Six

When Natalie came downstairs the next evening she discovered that Tony had already arrived. He and Tom were standing in the foyer in the midst of a discussion when she came out of her room and started down the stairway. Both men stopped talking and looked up.

She caught her breath. Tony wore a black suit that fit him like a glove, the white of his dress shirt showing up in a splendid contrast, emphasizing his tanned skin, black hair and eyes.

He looked wonderful to her, and from the look on his face as he watched her descend the stairs toward him, he was having a similar reaction to her.

She had chosen to wear a white dress with silver threads interwoven through the fabric so that the dress sparkled with every move she made. The style was simple so as not to detract from the beauty of the cloth. It swirled around her legs as she moved toward the two men.

"I'm sorry to keep you waiting, Tony. I wasn't aware you were here."

He glanced at Tom. "I just arrived. You look beautiful, Natalie. All you need are your angel wings."

She looked at Tom and winked. "I'm not sure I'm ready for my halo just yet. What do you think, Tom?"

In an unusual gesture, he put his arm around her and hugged her close to him. "I have to admit there's a glow about you, sis, that I haven't seen in a very long time. Who knows? Maybe the halo comes next.''

Surprised at his show of affection, she kissed him on the cheek. ''Where's Mother?''

''She hasn't come downstairs yet. I'm taking her over to some friends' home a little later.''

Tony picked up her coat and laid it across her shoulders, carefully lifting the hood so that it protected her head.

''I'm not sure when I'll be home, Tom,'' she began when Tom interrupted her.

''Don't worry about it. Just have a wonderful Christmas celebration, all right?''

She smiled. ''I will.'' Glancing at Tony, her smile widened. ''I know I will.''

It was already dark when they stepped outside. Once again a sense of déjà vu swept over her. The night was so clear that the stars seemed to be within reach. The air felt clean and fresh, and Natalie took a deep breath, as though to draw in some of the magic of the night.

Tony tucked her into the car before closing the door and joining her.

''Mama is so excited. She and Angela have been baking all day. Several of my aunts and uncles came over from the coast to join us. So the house will be full.'' He glanced over and grinned at her. ''As usual.''

They had to park several houses away from the D'Angelo home. Every window was brightly lit, and as they approached the front porch they heard the music, voices and laughter of happy people.

Just before he opened the door, Tony paused and placing his hands lightly on her shoulders, he leaned down and kissed her softly on the lips.

"Merry Christmas, Natalie."

She knew her face was flushed when they walked into the house. Everyone greeted them boisterously, teasing them unmercifully about arriving late. Within minutes Natalie felt as though she'd been embraced by every member of the clan as they hugged and kissed her, exclaiming how beautiful she looked. Tony never loosened his hold on her hand as they moved through the crowded rooms. Instead, he stood beside her grinning, refusing to respond to the teasing they were receiving. To his father he shrugged and said, "I was late getting away tonight."

His father patted his shoulder. "I know. This is a busy time for you."

The hours seemed to run together as the family gathered around the old upright piano while Serena D'Angelo played. Tony's father had a rich baritone voice and led the rest through several carols.

Even the small children joined in, their treble voices occasionally off-key but always enthusiastic.

Before Natalie realized the time, Tony was placing her coat around her once more. That was when she saw that the rest of the family members, Angela and Paul included, were gathering up coats and hats in order to go to the midnight services at the church.

There was no question about anyone riding with them, since the sports car only contained two seats. Tony wrapped his arm securely around Natalie, and they hurried to the car. Snowflakes had begun to fall all around them.

"The children will all be happy if this stuff sticks," Tony said as soon as they were on the way. "But right now it's fairly slick to be out driving."

The peaceful serenity of the night seemed to surround them as they drove slowly through the residential streets. Most people had gone to bed by now. For a moment Natalie felt as though she and Tony were the only people awake. The illusion dissipated when they pulled into the full parking lot at the church. Many people had chosen to spend this night in quiet contemplation of the meaning behind all of the festivities.

Tony and Natalie found places toward the back of the church and sat close together to give room to others arriving behind them.

Natalie had never dreamed that she would be able to reenact that night with Tony once again. Looking at him, she knew that there were vital changes now. They were both adults. They knew what they wanted in life. At least, she did. What Natalie realized as she sat there through the moving story of the very first Christmas was that what she wanted more than anything was to spend the rest of her life with the loving, tender, compassionate man beside her, to share many more moments like this one with him.

She could visualize the years to come when they would have children who would participate in the observance of Christmas, a family they would be able to share with and teach to appreciate what it meant to have been blessed with such love from God.

When the service was over they left the church without speaking. They drove to Lake Oswego in silence, although Natalie felt as though there were unseen carolers singing in the far distance, just out of range of her conscious hearing.

When they pulled up in front of the house, Natalie noticed that the snow had dusted the shrubs around the doorway, as though even they needed to be decorated in order to fully celebrate the occasion.

They entered the hallway, and Natalie noticed a light coming from upstairs. She looked around at Tony. "Did you mean to leave a light on?"

He helped her out of her coat and then took her hand. Leading her toward the stairway, he nodded. "Yes." When he started up the stairs, she followed.

He paused in the doorway of his bedroom and motioned for her to go inside.

A small Christmas tree sat on a table between the large picture windows that overlooked the lake. Twinkling lights blinked on and off. Gaily colored decorations hung on the tree. Perched at its point, a tiny angel with long blond hair and a white gown waited for them.

"When did you do this?" she asked in surprise.

"This afternoon. I wanted us to have our own special tree."

"What a lovely idea."

He walked over to the tree and picked up a small package. Without saying anything he handed it to her.

Natalie's hands were shaking so hard she wasn't sure she was going to be able to pull off the paper. When she finally did, she almost dropped the small case. Inside was a glittering ring, a sparkling blue stone surrounded by diamonds.

"Oh, Tony. It's beautiful."

"The color matches your eyes. I was told that it's called a London blue topaz. All I know is that I thought of you when I saw it."

He lifted it from the box, then slipped it on the third finger of her left hand. "Merry Christmas, love," he whispered, and kissed her.

When he loosened his hold a few minutes later, Natalie couldn't hide the tears in her eyes.

"What's wrong?"

"Nothing's wrong! Everything is so right I can't believe it. Tony, does this mean you want to start all over again? That we have a chance to build a life together?"

"Is that what you want?"

"More than I've ever wanted anything."

"Do you mean you're willing to move back to Portland?"

"I want to be with you, Tony, wherever that might be."

"Would you want to live here in this house?"

"If that's what you want."

He picked her up and carried her to the side of the bed. "That's what I want."

She watched as he loosened the unaccustomed tie around his neck and slipped off his suit jacket. Then she glanced down at the ring. "This time we're doing everything in order."

"What do you mean?"

Holding up her hand, she said, "The engagement ring first."

Tony paused as he unbuttoned the top two buttons of his shirt. "Well, not exactly." He turned away and walked toward the windows. "Do you remember that

I told you I made an agreement with your father six years ago?"

"To leave me alone?"

"Yes. To let you get on with your life and your education. I promised him that I would not do anything to influence you to come back to me." Without turning around he added, "I believe I kept that promise."

"Yes. You did. I never expected to hear from you again."

"You would have, at least indirectly, if at any time you had made any indication to your family that you were interested in another man."

"I don't understand."

Tony continued to stare out the window. "I agreed to leave you alone. In exchange, your father agreed not to have our marriage annulled."

She stared at his back in astonishment, trying to make some sense out of what he was saying.

"You mean—" she walked over to him, trying to see his face "—there was never an annulment?"

"That's right."

What he was saying was unbelievable. Did he mean that during all this time—while she was away at school and he was here—

"Tony?"

Slowly he turned to face her, his hands in his pants pockets, his expression guarded. "The marriage was valid, Natalie. Your father made sure of that. He hoped to find some way to get out of the agreement we made, so he had it all checked out."

"Then you and I are married."

He nodded.

"And no one ever told me."

"Your mother doesn't know. Only your father, Tom and I. Then after your father died..." His voice faded off.

"All this time Tom knew, and he never said a word?"

"No. He wanted to see if it was an infatuation with you. I promised him that if you ever met anyone else, I would immediately start proceedings to dissolve the marriage."

"I was never interested in anyone else."

"That's the only thing that has kept me going all these years, love. I got reports third hand—through your mother to Tom, then to me."

"So that's why you seem to know him so well."

"Not well. But we've stayed in touch. You see—" Once again he turned away, this time to the little tree that blinked so merrily beside the window. "You were my wife, and I wanted to be responsible for you. I insisted on paying all of your school expenses."

"You what! But that wasn't fair. My family had the money. You didn't."

"Maybe not at first," he admitted wryly, "but I was determined to show your family that I could do whatever it took to take care of you." His grin slowly appeared. "The hours I put in at work and school kept me too tired to think about anything else—like the fact that I had a wife that didn't know she was my wife. Like the fact that I didn't even know if you'd ever want me again. Like the fact that your refusal to return to Portland had almost convinced Tom that I was wasting my time and money in hopes of your wanting me."

"Oh, Tony," she cried, throwing herself into his arms. "If only I'd known! All these years we could have been together. All of these years so wasted."

"Not wasted. We both needed some time. Proving myself to your family made me more determined than ever to succeed. You had never treated me as the gardener's grandson, someone to look down on. I wasn't going to tolerate that treatment from your family."

She hugged him tightly, her cheek resting against the softness of his silk shirt. "Oh, Tony, I love you so much."

He sighed, his arms going convulsively around her. "There were nights when I would lie in bed wondering if I'd ever hear you say that again." He tilted her chin so that his mouth found hers, and all the longing, the uncertainty, the love that he'd carried within him for her all of these years seemed to pour from him, filling her heart and soul with gladness.

When the kiss could no longer properly express what he was feeling, Tony picked her up once more, this time laying her tenderly on the bed without breaking the kiss. He came down beside her, his restless hands exploring her, loving and adoring her.

All of the uncertainty she had experienced since seeing him that day at the mall disappeared in the passionate intensity of his kiss. She couldn't seem to get close enough to him, and Natalie hastily tugged at the buttons on his shirt, trying to reach the warm flesh hidden beneath the silk.

She felt the zipper at the back of her dress move down, and she willingly moved away from him long enough to remove the beautiful gown. Tony pulled away from her in order to slide the silken underwear from her body, so that she was bathed in the twinkling light coming from the tree.

"My Christmas angel. Happy anniversary, darling," he whispered. He quickly dispensed with the remainder of his clothes and stretched out beside her once more.

Natalie could more readily see the changes that had taken place in his body—the wide chest and heavy shoulders were revealed to her in all their silken splendor. She followed the curve of his chest down to his waist, then smoothed her hand across his abdomen and down his thigh. His skin rippled beneath her touch, and he pulled her over until she lay on top of him.

"Do you have any idea what you're doing to me, woman?" he groaned.

"I seem to be having a similar reaction," she admitted.

"Six years is a long time to wait, you know."

"I know that. I'm not asking how you spent those years, love. How can I possibly ask?"

"But I can answer. I didn't want anyone but you, Natalie. My thoughts and dreams have always been filled with you. I never wanted anyone but you. Never." His hands encircled her head and gently brought it down to him so that his mouth could touch hers. He ran his tongue along the surface of her lips, then plunged deeply inside—taking possession.

There was never any doubt how his body reacted to her nearness, and Natalie could no longer ignore her position on top of him. Raising herself slightly, she moved so that she could enfold and absorb him, her action causing him to gasp at the pleasure of joining with her once more.

Fiercely he held her as she moved over him, at long last able to enact some of her many fantasies over the years.

Eventually she collapsed on his chest, too weak to continue. Tony rolled so that she was tucked beneath him, bringing her to repeated peaks until at long last he joined her in that wonderful feeling of total satiation.

Not wanting to crush her, he stretched out beside her, holding her close. Her eyes drifted shut, then popped open again. She didn't want to waste a moment of this time.

The Christmas angel kept a watchful eye over the proceedings, her kindly smile indicating that all was well. Once again the magic of Christmas had brought to Natalie her heart's desire.

This time she knew it would last forever.

"Are you awake?" Tony whispered a few minutes later.

"Mmm-hmm."

"Are you hungry?"

"Not really, why?"

"I thought we could raid the refrigerator. I stocked up on everything I could think of before I left here today."

"Do you think I should call Tom so he and Mother don't worry about me? The roads are going to be treacherous tonight."

With his forefinger, Tony traced a trail from her chin down her throat, between her breasts and finally paused at her abdomen. "Tom knew you weren't coming back home tonight."

"Is that what you two were talking about in the foyer?"

"Yes. He told me that there was no reason not to tell you the truth now. I'd already decided I couldn't wait any longer, anyway. Whatever the outcome, you had to know."

"I can't believe that both of you kept this from me all these years."

"Your mother is going to be the one in shock. She never knew what had happened. Your father told her that he had found you at my parents' home, that you'd stayed overnight with Angela."

"And she believed that, as upset as I was?"

"I suppose. So now we're going to have to explain to her why you aren't going to be home until a few days after Christmas."

She ran her fingers through his black curls. "A few days?"

"I don't intend to let you out of my bed any longer than I can help it. Why do you suppose I'm offering food? I want you to keep your strength up."

"What about you?"

"I've been doing that for six years, love." His slow kiss made it clear that he was more than willing to demonstrate.

Natalie settled contentedly into his arms. In a contest of this nature, there were definitely no losers.

With Christmas magic, anything was possible.

*   *   *   *   *

SWEET POTATO-BERRY BAKE
Preparation time: 30 minutes

2 17 oz cans sweet potatoes, halved and drained
1 cup fresh cranberries
¼ cup chopped pecans
½ cup orange marmalade

Preheat oven to 350° F.

Place sweet potatoes in a 10″ × 6″ baking dish. Top with berries and nuts. Dot with marmalade. Bake for 30 minutes. Serve piping hot.

As Annette told us it would, "The sweet-and-sour mix makes a fantastic taste treat and had the family going back for seconds."

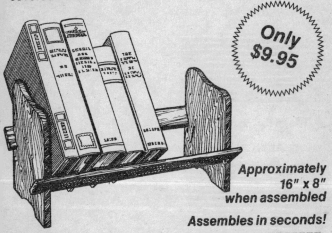

We hope you enjoyed this Christmas story. This story and three other great stories are featured in *Silhouette Christmas Stories 1988*, just released in bookstores and other outlets where books are sold.